The Light Princess

By George MacDonald

A Digireads.com Book
Digireads.com Publishing
16212 Riggs Rd
Stilwell, KS, 66085

The Light Princess
By George MacDonald
ISBN: 1-4209-3096-6

Please visit *www.digireads.com*

1.

What! No Children?

Once upon a time, so long ago that I have quite forgotten the date, there lived a king and queen who had no children.

And the king said to himself, "All the queens of my acquaintance have children, some three, some seven, and some as many as twelve; and my queen has not one. I feel ill-used." So he made up his mind to be cross with his wife about it. But she bore it all like a good patient queen as she was. Then the king grew very cross indeed. But the queen pretended to take it all as a joke, and a very good one too.

"Why don't you have any daughters, at least?" said he. "I don't say sons; that might be too much to expect."

"I am sure, dear king, I am very sorry," said the queen.

"So you ought to be," retorted the king; "you are not going to make a virtue of that, surely."

But he was not an ill-tempered king, and in any matter of less moment would have let the queen have her own way with all his heart. This, however, was an affair of state.

The queen smiled.

"You must have patience with a lady, you know, dear king," said she.

She was, indeed, a very nice queen, and heartily sorry that she could not oblige the king immediately.

2.

Won't I, Just?

The king tried to have patience, but he succeeded very badly. It was more than he deserved, therefore, when, at last, the queen gave him a daughter—as lovely a little princess as ever cried.

The day drew near when the infant must be christened. The king wrote all the invitations with his own hand. Of course somebody was forgotten. Now it does not generally matter if somebody is forgotten, only you must mind who.

Unfortunately, the king forgot without intending to forget; and so the chance fell upon the Princess Makemnoit, which was awkward. For the princess was the king's own sister; and he ought not to have forgotten her. But she had made herself so disagreeable to the old king, their father, that he had forgotten her in making his will; and so it was no wonder that her brother forgot her in writing his invitations. But poor relations don't do anything to keep you in mind of them. Why don't they? The king could not see into the garret she lived in, could he?

She was a sour, spiteful creature. The wrinkles of contempt crossed the wrinkles of peevishness, and made her face as full of wrinkles as a pat of butter. If ever a king could be justified in forgetting anybody, this king was justified in forgetting his sister, even at a christening. She looked very odd, too. Her forehead was as large as all the rest of her face, and projected over it like a precipice. When she was angry, her little eyes flashed blue. When she hated anybody, they shone yellow and green. What they looked like when she loved anybody, I do not know; for I never heard of her loving anybody but herself, and I do not think she could have managed that if she had not somehow got used to herself. But what made it highly imprudent in the king to forget her was that she was awfully clever. In fact, she was a witch; and when she bewitched anybody, he very soon had enough of it; for she beat all the wicked fairies in wickedness, and all the clever ones in cleverness. She despised all the modes we read of in history, in which offended fairies and witches have taken their revenges; and therefore, after waiting and waiting in vain for an invitation, she made up her mind at last to go without one, and make the whole family miserable, like a princess as she was.

So she put on her best gown, went to the palace, was kindly received by the happy monarch, who forgot that he had forgotten her, and took her place in the procession to the royal chapel. When they were all gathered about the font, she contrived to get next to it, and throw something into the water; after which she maintained a very respectful demeanour till the water was applied to the child's face. But at that moment she turned round in her place three times, and muttered the following words, loud enough for those beside her to hear:—

> *"Light of spirit, by my charms,*
> *Light of body, every part,*
> *Never weary human arms—*
> *Only crush thy parents' heart!"*

They all thought she had lost her wits, and was repeating some foolish nursery rhyme; but a shudder went through the whole of them notwithstanding. The baby, on the contrary, began to laugh and crow; while the nurse gave a start and a smothered cry, for she thought she was struck with paralysis: she could not feel the baby in her arms. But she clasped it tight and said nothing.

The mischief was done.

3.

She Can't Be Ours.

Her atrocious aunt had deprived the child of all her gravity. If you ask me how this was effected, I answer, "In the easiest way in the world. She had only to destroy gravitation." For the princess was a philosopher, and knew all the ins and outs of the laws of gravitation as well as the ins and outs of her boot-lace. And being a witch as well, she could abrogate those laws in a moment; or at least so clog their wheels and rust their bearings, that they would not work at all. But we have more to do with what followed than with how it was done.

The first awkwardness that resulted from this unhappy privation was, that the moment the nurse began to float the baby up and down, she flew from her arms towards the ceiling. Happily, the resistance of the air brought her ascending career to a close within a foot of it. There she remained, horizontal as when she left her nurse's arms, kicking and laughing amazingly. The nurse in terror flew to the bell, and begged the footman, who answered it, to bring up the house-steps directly. Trembling in every limb, she climbed upon the steps, and had to stand upon the very top, and reach up, before she could catch the floating tail of the baby's long clothes.

When the strange fact came to be known, there was a terrible commotion in the palace. The occasion of its discovery by the king was naturally a repetition of the nurse's experience. Astonished that he felt no weight when the child was laid in his arms, he began to wave her up and not down, for she slowly ascended to the ceiling as before, and there remained floating in perfect comfort and satisfaction, as was testified by her peals of tiny laughter. The king stood staring up in speechless amazement, and trembled so that his beard shook like grass in the wind. At last, turning to the queen, who was just as horror-struck as himself, he said, gasping, staring, and stammering,—

"She can't be ours, queen!"

Now the queen was much cleverer than the king, and had begun already to suspect that "this effect defective came by cause."

"I am sure she is ours," answered she. "But we ought to have taken better care of her at the christening. People who were never invited ought not to have been present."

"Oh, ho!" said the king, tapping his forehead with his forefinger, "I have it all. I've found her out. Don't you see it, queen? Princess Makemnoit has bewitched her." "That's just what I say," answered the queen.

"I beg your pardon, my love; I did not hear you.—John! bring the steps I get on my throne with."

For he was a little king with a great throne, like many other kings.

The throne-steps were brought, and set upon the dining-table, and John got upon the top of them. But he could not reach the little princess, who lay like a baby-laughter-cloud in the air, exploding continuously. "Take the tongs, John," said his Majesty; and getting up on the table, he handed them to him.

John could reach the baby now, and the little princess was handed down by the tongs.

4.

Where Is She?

One fine summer day, a month after these her first adventures, during which time she had been very carefully watched, the princess was lying on the bed in the queen's own chamber, fast asleep. One of the windows was open, for it was noon, and the day was so sultry that the little girl was wrapped in nothing less ethereal than slumber itself. The queen came into the room, and not observing that the baby was on the bed, opened another window. A frolicsome fairy wind, which had been watching for a chance of mischief, rushed in at the one window, and taking its way over the bed where the child was lying, caught her up, and rolling and floating her along like a piece of flue, or a dandelion seed, carried her with it through the opposite window, and away. The queen went down-stairs, quite ignorant of the loss she had herself occasioned.

When the nurse returned, she supposed that her Majesty had carried her off, and, dreading a scolding, delayed making inquiry about her. But hearing nothing, she grew uneasy, and went at length to the queen's boudoir, where she found her Majesty.

"Please, your Majesty, shall I take the baby?" said she.

"Where is she?" asked the queen.

"Please forgive me. I know it was wrong."

"What do you mean?" said the queen, looking grave.

"Oh! don't frighten me, your Majesty!" exclaimed the nurse, clasping her hands.

The queen saw that something was amiss, and fell down in a faint. The nurse rushed about the palace, screaming, "My baby! my baby!"

Every one ran to the queen's room. But the queen could give no orders. They soon found out, however, that the princess was missing, and in a moment the palace was like a beehive in a garden; and in one minute more the queen was brought to herself by a great shout and a clapping of hands. They had found the princess fast asleep under a rose-bush, to which the elvish little wind-puff had carried her, finishing its mischief by shaking a shower of red rose-leaves all over the little white sleeper. Startled by the noise the servants made, she woke, and, furious with glee, scattered the rose- leaves in all directions, like a shower of spray in the sunset.

She was watched more carefully after this, no doubt; yet it would be endless to relate all the odd incidents resulting from this peculiarity of the young princess. But there never was a baby in a house, not to say a palace, that kept the household in such constant good humour, at least below- stairs. If it was not easy for her nurses to hold her, at least she made neither their arms nor their hearts ache. And she was so nice to play at ball with! There was positively no danger of letting her fall. They might throw her down, or knock her down, or push her down, but couldn't let her down. It is true, they might let her fly into the fire or the coal-hole, or through the window; but none of these accidents had happened as yet. If you heard peals of laughter resounding from some unknown region, you might be sure enough of the cause. Going down into the kitchen, or the room, you would find Jane and Thomas, and Robert and Susan, all and sum, playing at ball with the little princess. She was the ball herself, and did not enjoy it the less for that. Away she went, flying from one to another, screeching with laughter. And the servants loved the ball itself better even than the game. But they had to take some care how they threw her, for if she received an upward direction, she would never come down again without being fetched.

5.

What Is to Be Done?

But above-stairs it was different. One day, for instance, after breakfast, the king went into his counting-house, and counted out his money. The operation gave him no pleasure.

"To think," said he to himself, "that every one of these gold sovereigns weighs a quarter of an ounce, and my real, live, flesh-and-blood princess weighs nothing at all!"

And he hated his gold sovereigns, as they lay with a broad smile of self-satisfaction all over their yellow faces.

The queen was in the parlour, eating bread and honey. But at the second mouthful she burst out crying, and could not swallow it.

The king heard her sobbing. Glad of anybody, but especially of his queen, to quarrel with, he clashed his gold sovereigns into his money-box, clapped his crown on his head, and rushed into the parlour.

"What is all this about?" exclaimed he. "What are you crying for, queen?"

"I can't eat it," said the queen, looking ruefully at the honey-pot.

"-No wonder!" retorted the king. "You've just eaten your breakfast —two turkey eggs, and three anchovies."

"Oh, that's not it!" sobbed her Majesty. "It's my child, my child!"

"Well, what's the matter with your child? She's neither up the chimney nor down the draw-well. Just hear her laughing."

Yet the king could not help a sigh, which he tried to turn into a cough, saying—

"It is a good thing to be light-hearted, I am sure, whether she be ours or not."

"It is a bad thing to be light-headed," answered the queen, looking with prophetic soul far into the future.

"'Tis a good thing to be light-handed," said the king.

"'Tis a bad thing to be light-fingered," answered the queen.

"'Tis a good thing to be light-footed," said the king.

"'Tis a bad thing—" began the queen; but the king interrupted her.

"In fact," said he, with the tone of one who concludes an argument in which he has had only imaginary opponents, and in which, therefore, he has come off triumphant—"in fact, it is a good thing altogether to be light-bodied."

"But it is a bad thing altogether to be light- minded," retorted the queen, who was beginning to lose her temper.

This last answer quite discomfited his Majesty, who turned on his heel, and betook himself to his counting-house again. But he was not half-way towards it, when the voice of his queen overtook him.

"And it's a bad thing to be light-haired," screamed she, determined to have more last words, now that her spirit was roused.

The queen's hair was black as night; and the king's had been, and his daughter's was, golden as morning. But it was not this reflection on his hair that arrested him; it was the double use of the word light. For the king hated all witticisms, and punning especially. And besides, he could not tell whether the queen meant light-haired or light-heired; for why might she not aspirate her vowels when she was exasperated herself?

He turned upon his other heel, and rejoined her. She looked angry still, because she knew that she was guilty, or, what was much the same, knew that he thought so.

"My dear queen," said he, "duplicity of any sort is exceedingly objectionable between married people of any rank, not to say kings and queens; and the most objectionable form duplicity can assume is that of punning."

"There!" said the queen, "I never made a jest, but I broke it in the making. I am the most unfortunate woman in the world!"

She looked so rueful, that the king took her in his arms; and they sat down to consult.

"Can you bear this?" said the king.

"No, I can't," said the queen.

"Well, what's to be done?" said the king.

"I'm sure I don't know," said the queen. "But might you not try an apology?"

"To my old sister, I suppose you mean?" said the king.

"Yes," said the queen.

"Well, I don't mind," said the king.

So he went the next morning to the house of the princess, and, making a very humble apology, begged her to undo the spell. But the princess declared, with a grave face, that she knew nothing at all about it. Her eyes, however, shone pink, which was a sign that she was happy. She advised the king and queen to have patience, and to mend their ways. The king returned disconsolate. The queen tried to comfort him.

"We will wait till she is older. She may then be able to suggest something herself. She will know at least how she feels, and explain things to us."

"But what if she should marry?" exclaimed the king, in sudden consternation at the idea.

"Well, what of that?" rejoined the queen. "Just think! If she were to have children! In the course of a hundred years the air might be as full of floating children as of gossamers in autumn."

"That is no business of ours," replied the queen. "Besides, by that time they will have learned to take care of themselves."

A sigh was the king's only answer.

He would have consulted the court physicians; but he was afraid they would try experiments upon her.

6.

She Laughs Too Much.

Meantime, notwithstanding awkward occurrences, and griefs that she brought upon her parents, the little princess laughed and grew—not fat, but plump and tall. She reached the age of seventeen, without having fallen into any worse scrape than a chimney; by rescuing her from which, a little bird-nesting urchin got fame and a black face. Nor, thoughtless as she was, had she committed anything worse than laughter at everybody and everything that came in her way. When she was told, for the sake of experiment, that General Clanrunfort was cut to pieces with all his troops, she laughed; when she heard that the enemy was on his way to besiege her papa's capital, she laughed hugely; but when she was told that the city would certainly be abandoned to the mercy of the enemy's soldiery—why, then she laughed immoderately. She never could be brought to see the serious side of anything. When her mother cried, she said,—

"What queer faces mamma makes! And she squeezes water out of her cheeks? Funny mamma!"

And when her papa stormed at her, she laughed, and danced round and round him, clapping her hands, and crying—

"Do it again, papa. Do it again! It's such fun! Dear, funny papa!"

And if he tried to catch her, she glided from him in an instant, not in the least afraid of him, but thinking it part of the game not to be caught. With one push of her foot, she would be floating in the air above his head; or she would go dancing backwards and forwards and sideways, like a great butterfly. It happened several times, when her father and mother were holding a consultation about her in private, that they were interrupted by vainly repressed outbursts of laughter over their heads; and looking up with indignation, saw her floating at full length in the air above them, whence she regarded them with the most comical appreciation of the position.

One day an awkward accident happened. The princess had come out upon the lawn with one of her attendants, who held her by the hand. Spying her father at the other side of the lawn, she snatched her hand from the maid's, and sped across to him. Now when she wanted to run alone, her custom was to catch up a stone in each hand, so that she might come down again after a bound. Whatever she wore as part of her attire had no effect in this way: even gold, when it thus became as it were a part of herself, lost all its weight for the time. But whatever she only held in her hands retained its downward tendency. On this occasion she could see nothing to catch up but a huge toad, that was walking across the lawn as if he had a hundred years to do it in. Not knowing what disgust meant, for this was one of her peculiarities, she snatched up the toad and bounded away. She had almost reached her father, and he was holding out his arms to receive her, and take from her lips the kiss which hovered on them like a butterfly on a rosebud, when a puff of wind blew her aside into the arms of a young page, who had just been receiving a message from his Majesty. Now it was no great peculiarity in the princess that, once she was set agoing, it always cost her time and trouble to check herself. On this occasion there was no time. She must kiss-and she kissed the page. She did not mind it much; for she had no shyness in her composition; and she knew, besides, that she could not help it. So she only laughed, like a musical box. The poor page fared the worst. For the princess, trying to correct the unfortunate tendency of the kiss, put out her hands to keep her off the page; so that, along with the kiss, he received, on the other cheek, a slap with the huge black toad, which she poked right into his eye. He tried to laugh, too, but the attempt resulted in such an odd contortion of countenance, as showed that there was no danger of his pluming himself on the kiss. As for the king, his dignity was greatly hurt, and he did not speak to the page for a whole month.

I may here remark that it was very amusing to see her run, if her mode of progression could properly be called running. For first she would make a bound; then, having alighted, she would run a few steps, and make another bound. Sometimes she would fancy she had reached the ground before she actually had, and her feet would go backwards and forwards, running upon nothing at all, like those of a chicken on its back. Then she would laugh like the very spirit of fun; only in her laugh there was something missing. What it was, I find myself unable to describe. I think it was a certain tone, depending upon the possibility of sorrow—*morbidezza*, perhaps. She never smiled.

7.

Try Metaphysics.

After a long avoidance of the painful subject, the king and queen resolved to hold a council of three upon it; and so they sent for the princess. In she came, sliding and flitting and gliding from one piece of furniture to another, and put herself at last in an armchair, in a sitting posture. Whether she could be said to sit, seeing she received no support from the seat of the chair, I do not pretend to determine.

"My dear child," said the king, "you must be aware by this time that you are not exactly like other people."

"Oh, you dear funny papa! I have got a nose, and two eyes, and all the rest. So have you. So has mamma."

"Now be serious, my dear, for once," said the queen.

"No, thank you, mamma; I had rather not."

"Would you not like to be able to walk like other people?" said the king. "No indeed, I should think not. You only crawl. You are such slow coaches!"

"How do you feel, my child?" he resumed, after a pause of discomfiture.

"Quite well, thank you."

"I mean, what do you feel like?"

"Like nothing at all, that I know of."

"You must feel like something."

"I feel like a princess with such a funny papa, and such a dear pet of a queen-mamma!"

"Now really!" began the queen; but the princess interrupted her.

"Oh Yes," she added, "I remember. I have a curious feeling sometimes, as if I were the only person that had any sense in the whole world."

She had been trying to behave herself with dignity; but now she burst into a violent fit of laughter, threw herself backwards over the chair, and went rolling about the floor in an ecstasy of enjoyment. The king picked her up easier than one does a down quilt, and replaced her in her former relation to the chair. The exact preposition expressing this relation I do not happen to know.

"Is there nothing you wish for?" resumed the king, who had learned by this time that it was useless to be angry with her.

"Oh, you dear papa!—yes," answered she.

"What is it, my darling?"

"I have been longing for it—oh, such a time!—ever since last night." "Tell me what it is."

"Will you promise to let me have it?"

The king was on the point of saying Yes, but the wiser queen checked him with a single motion of her head. "Tell me what it is first," said he.

"No no. Promise first."

"I dare not. What is it?"

"Mind, I hold you to your promise.—It is—to be tied to the end of a string—a very long string indeed, and be flown like a kite. Oh, such fun! I would rain rose-water, and hail sugar-plums, and snow whipped-cream, and—and—and—"

A fit of laughing checked her; and she would have been off again over the floor, had not the king started up and caught her just in time. Seeing nothing but talk could be got out of her, he rang the bell, and sent her away with two of her ladies-in-waiting.

"Now, queen," he said, turning to her Majesty, "what IS to be done?"

"There is but one thing left," answered she. "Let us consult the college of Metaphysicians."

"Bravo!" cried the king; "we will."

Now at the head of this college were two very wise Chinese philosophers-by name Hum-Drum, and Kopy-Keck. For them the king sent; and straightway they came. In a long speech he communicated to them what they knew very well already—as who did not?—namely, the peculiar condition of his daughter in relation to the globe on which she dwelt; and requested them to consult together as to what might be the cause and probable cure of her *infirmity*. The king laid stress upon the word, but failed to discover his own pun. The queen laughed; but Hum-Drum and Kopy-Keck heard with humility and retired in silence.

The consultation consisted chiefly in propounding and supporting, for the thousandth time, each his favourite theories. For the condition of the princess afforded delightful scope for the discussion of every question arising from the division of thought-in fact, of all the Metaphysics of the Chinese Empire. But it is only justice to say that they did not altogether neglect the discussion of the practical question, what was to be done.

Hum-Drum was a Materialist, and Kopy-Keck was a Spiritualist. The former was slow and sententious; the latter was quick and flighty: the latter had generally the first word; the former the last.

"I reassert my former assertion," began Kopy-Keck, with a plunge. "There is not a fault in the princess, body or soul; only they are wrong put together. Listen to me now, Hum-Drum, and I will tell you in brief what I think. Don't speak. Don't answer me. I won't hear you till I have done.—At that decisive moment, when souls seek their appointed habitations, two eager souls met, struck, rebounded, lost their way, and arrived each at the wrong place. The soul of the princess was one of those, and she went far astray. She does not belong by rights to this world at all, but to some other planet, probably Mercury. Her proclivity to her true sphere destroys all the natural influence which this orb would otherwise possess over her corporeal frame. She cares for nothing here. There is no relation between her and this world.

"She must therefore be taught, by the sternest compulsion, to take an interest in the earth as the earth. She must study every department of its history—its animal history; its vegetable history; its mineral history; its social history; its moral history; its political history, its scientific history; its literary history; its musical history; its artistical history; above all, its metaphysical history. She must begin with the Chinese dynasty and end with Japan. But first of all she must study geology, and especially the history of the extinct races of animals-their natures, their habits, their loves, their hates, their revenges. She must—"

"Hold, h-o-o-old!" roared Hum-Drum. "It is certainly my turn now. My rooted and insubvertible conviction is, that the causes of the anomalies evident in the princess's condition are strictly and solely physical. But that is only tantamount to acknowledging that they exist. Hear my opinion.—From some cause or other, of no importance to our inquiry, the motion of her heart has been reversed. That remarkable combination of the suction and the force-pump works the wrong way-I mean in the case of the unfortunate princess: it draws in where it should force out, and forces out where it should draw in. The offices of the auricles and the ventricles are subverted. The blood is sent forth by the veins, and returns by the arteries. Consequently it is running the wrong way through all her corporeal organism—lungs and all. Is it then at all mysterious, seeing that such is the case, that on the other particular of gravitation as well, she should differ from normal humanity? My proposal for the cure is this:—

"Phlebotomize until she is reduced to the last point of safety. Let it be effected, if necessary, in a warm bath. When she is reduced to a state of perfect asphyxy, apply a ligature to the left ankle, drawing it as tight as the bone will bear. Apply, at the same moment, another of equal tension around the right wrist. By means of plates constructed for the purpose, place the other foot and hand under the receivers of two air-pumps. Exhaust the receivers. Exhibit a pint of French brandy, and await the result."

"Which would presently arrive in the form of grim Death," said Kopy-Keck.

"If it should, she would yet die in doing our duty," retorted Hum-Drum.

But their Majesties had too much tenderness for their volatile offspring to subject her to either of the schemes of the equally unscrupulous philosophers. Indeed, the most complete knowledge of the laws of nature would have been unserviceable in her case; for it was impossible to classify her. She was a fifth imponderable body, sharing all the other properties of the ponderable.

8.

Try a Drop of Water.

Perhaps the best thing for the princess would have been to fall in love. But how a princess who had no gravity could fall into anything is a difficulty—perhaps *the* difficulty.

As for her own feelings on the subject, she did not even know that there was such a beehive of honey and stings to be fallen into. But now I come to mention another curious fact about her.

The palace was built on the shores of the loveliest lake in the world; and the princess loved this lake more than father or mother. The root of this preference no doubt, although the princess did not recognise it as such, was, that the moment she got into it, she recovered the natural right of which she had been so wickedly deprived—namely, gravity. Whether this was owing to the fact that water had been employed as the means of conveying the injury, I do not know. But it is certain that she could swim and dive like the duck that her old nurse said she was. The manner in which this alleviation of her misfortune was discovered was as follows.

One summer evening, during the carnival of the country, she had been taken upon the lake by the king and queen, in the royal barge. They were accompanied by many of the courtiers in a fleet of little boats. In the middle of the lake she wanted to get into the lord chancellor's barge, for his daughter, who was a great favourite with her, was in it with her father. Now though the old king rarely condescended to make light of his misfortune, yet, Happening on this occasion to be in a particularly good humour, as the barges approached each other, he caught up the princess to throw her into the chancellor's barge. He lost his balance, however, and, dropping into the bottom of the barge, lost his hold of his daughter; not, however, before imparting to her the downward tendency of his own person, though in a somewhat different direction; for, as the king fell into the boat, she fell into the water. With a burst of delighted laughter she disappeared in the lake. A cry of horror ascended from the boats. They had never seen the princess go down before. Half the men were under water in a moment; but they had all, one after another, come up to the surface again for breath, when—tinkle, tinkle, babble, and gush! came the princess's laugh over the water from far away. There she was, swimming like a swan. Nor would she come out for king or queen, chancellor or daughter. She was perfectly obstinate.

But at the same time she seemed more sedate than usual. Perhaps that was because a great pleasure spoils laughing. At all events, after this, the passion of her life was to get into the water, and she was always the better behaved and the more beautiful the more she had of it. Summer and winter it was quite the same; only she could not stay so long in the water when they had to break the ice to let her in. Any day, from morning till evening in summer, she might be descried—a streak of white in the blue water—lying as still as the shadow of a cloud, or shooting along like a dolphin; disappearing, and coming up again far off, just where one did not expect her. She would have been in the lake of a night, too, if she could have had her way; for the balcony of her window overhung a deep pool in it; and through a shallow reedy passage she could have swum out into the wide wet water, and no one would have been any the wiser. Indeed, when she happened to wake in the moonlight she could hardly resist the temptation. But there was the sad difficulty of getting into it. She had as great a dread of the air as some children have of the water. For the slightest gust of wind would blow her away; and a gust might arise in the stillest moment. And if she gave herself a push towards the water and just failed of reaching it, her situation would be dreadfully awkward, irrespective of the wind; for at best there she would have to remain, suspended in her nightgown, till she was seen and angled for by someone from the window.

"Oh! if I had my gravity," thought she, contemplating the water, "I would flash off this balcony like a long white sea-bird, headlong into the darling wetness. Heigh-ho!"

This was the only consideration that made her wish to be like other people.

Another reason for her being fond of the water was that in it alone she enjoyed any freedom. For she could not walk out without a cortege, consisting in part of a troop of light horse, for fear of the liberties which the wind might take with her. And the king grew more apprehensive with increasing years, till at last he would not allow her to walk abroad at all without some twenty silken cords fastened to as many parts of her dress, and held by twenty noblemen. Of course horseback was out of the question. But she bade good-by to all this ceremony when she got into the water.

And so remarkable were its effects upon her, especially in restoring her for the time to the ordinary human gravity, that Hum-Drum and Kopy-Keck agreed in recommending the king to bury her alive for three years; in the hope that, as the water did her so much good, the earth would do her yet more. But the king had some vulgar prejudices against the experiment, and would not give his consent. Foiled in this, they yet agreed in another recommendation; which, seeing that one imported his opinions from China and the other from Thibet, was very remarkable indeed. They argued that, if water of external origin and application could be so efficacious, water from a deeper source might work a perfect cure; in short, that if the poor afflicted princess could by any means be made to cry, she might recover her lost gravity.

But how was this to be brought about? Therein lay all the difficulty—to meet which the philosophers were not wise enough. To make the princess cry was as impossible as to make her weigh. They sent for a professional beggar; commanded him to prepare his most touching oracle of woe; helped him out of the court charade box, to whatever he wanted for dressing up, and promised great rewards in the event of his success. But it was all in vain. She listened to the mendicant artist's story, and gazed at his marvellous make up, till she could contain herself no longer, and went into the most undignified contortions for relief, shrieking, positively screeching with laughter.

When she had a little recovered herself, she ordered her attendants to drive him away, and not give him a single copper; whereupon his look of mortified discomfiture wrought her punishment and his revenge, for it sent her into violent hysterics, from which she was with difficulty recovered.

But so anxious was the king that the suggestion should have a fair trial, that he put himself in a rage one day, and, rushing up to her room, gave her an awful whipping. Yet not a tear would flow. She looked grave, and her laughing sounded uncommonly like screaming—that was all. The good old tyrant, though he put on his best gold spectacles to look, could not discover the smallest cloud in the serene blue of her eyes.

9.

Put Me in Again.

It must have been about this time that the son of a king, who lived a thousand miles from Lagobel set out to look for the daughter of a queen. He travelled far and wide, but as sure as he found a princess, he found some fault in her. Of course he could not marry a mere woman, however beautiful; and there was no princess to be found worthy of him. Whether the prince was so near perfection that he had a right to demand perfection itself, I cannot pretend to say. All I know is, that he was a fine, handsome, brave, generous, well-bred, and well-behaved youth, as all princes are.

In his wanderings he had come across some reports about our princess; but as everybody said she was bewitched, he never dreamed that she could bewitch him. For what indeed could a prince do with a princess that had lost her gravity? Who could tell what she might not lose next? She might lose her visibility, or her tangibility; or, in short, the power of making impressions upon the radical sensorium; so that he should never be able to tell whether she was dead or alive. Of course he made no further inquiries about her. One day he lost sight of his retinue in a great forest. These forests are very useful in delivering princes from their courtiers, like a sieve that keeps back the bran. Then the princes get away to follow their fortunes. In this way they have the advantage of the princesses, who are forced to marry before they have had a bit of fun. I wish our princesses got lost in a forest sometimes.

One lovely evening, after wandering about for many days, he found that he was approaching the outskirts of this forest; for the trees had got so thin that he could see the sunset through them; and he soon came upon a kind of heath. Next he came upon signs of human neighbourhood; but by this time it was getting late, and there was nobody in the fields to direct him.

After travelling for another hour, his horse, quite worn out with long labour and lack of food, fell, and was unable to rise again. So he continued his journey on foot. At length he entered another wood—not a wild forest, but a civilized wood, through which a footpath led him to the side of a lake. Along this path the prince pursued his way through the gathering darkness. Suddenly he paused, and listened. Strange sounds came across the water. It was, in fact, the princess laughing. Now there was something odd in her laugh, as I have already hinted; for the hatching of a real hearty laugh requires the incubation of gravity; and perhaps this was how the prince mistook the laughter for screaming. Looking over the lake, he saw something white in the water; and, in an instant, he had torn off his tunic, kicked off his sandals, and plunged in. He soon reached the white object, and found that it was a woman. There was not light enough to show that she was a princess, but quite enough to show that she was a lady, for it does not want much light to see that.

Now I cannot tell how it came about,—whether she pretended to be drowning, or whether he frightened her, or caught her so as to embarrass her,—but certainly he brought her to shore in a fashion ignominious to a swimmer, and more nearly drowned than she had ever expected to be; for the water had got into her throat as often as she had tried to speak.

At the place to which he bore her, the bank was only a foot or two above the water; so he gave her a strong lift out of the water, to lay her on the bank. But, her gravitation ceasing the moment she left the water, away she went up into the air, scolding and screaming.

"You naughty, *naughty*, NAUGHTY, NAUGHTY man!" she cried.

No one had ever succeeded in putting her into a passion before.—When the prince saw her ascend, he thought he must have been bewitched, and have mistaken a great swan for a lady. But the princess caught hold of the topmost cone upon a lofty fir. This came off; but she caught at another; and, in fact, stopped herself by gathering cones, dropping them as the stalks gave way. The prince, meantime, stood in the water, staring, and forgetting to get out. But the princess disappearing, he scrambled on shore, and went in the direction of the tree. There he found her climbing down one of the branches towards the stem. But in the darkness of the wood, the prince continued in some bewilderment as to what the phenomenon could be; until, reaching the ground, and seeing him standing there, she caught hold of him, and said,—

"I'll tell papa."

"Oh no, you won't!" returned the prince.

"Yes, I will," she persisted. "What business had you to pull me down out of the water, and throw me to the bottom of the air? I never did you any harm."

"Pardon me. I did not mean to hurt you."

"I don't believe you have any brains; and that is a worse loss than your wretched gravity. I pity you.'

The prince now saw that he had come upon the bewitched princess, and had already offended her. But before he could think what to say next, she burst out angrily, giving a stamp with her foot that would have sent her aloft again but for the hold she had of his arm,—

"Put me up directly."

"Put you up where, you beauty?" asked the prince.

He had fallen in love with her almost, already; for her anger made her more charming than any one else had ever beheld her; and, as far as he could see, which certainly was not far, she had not a single fault about her, except, of course, that she had not any gravity. No prince, however, would judge of a princess by weight. The loveliness of her foot he would hardly estimate by the depth of the impression it could make in mud.

"Put you up where, you beauty?" asked the prince.

"In the water, you stupid!" answered the princess.

"Come, then," said the prince.

The condition of her dress, increasing her usual difficulty in walking, compelled her to cling to him; and he could hardly persuade himself that he was not in a delightful dream, notwithstanding the torrent of musical abuse with which she overwhelmed him. The prince being therefore in no hurry, they came upon the lake at quite another part, where the bank was twenty-five feet high at least; and when they had reached the edge, he turned towards the princess, and said,—

"How am I to put you in?" "That is your business," she answered, quite snappishly. "You took me out—put me in again."

"Very well," said the prince; and, catching her up in his arms, he sprang with her from the rock. The princess had just time to give one delighted shriek of laughter before the water closed over them. When they came to the surface, she found that, for a moment or two, she could not even laugh, for she had gone down with such a rush, that it was with difficulty she recovered her breath. The instant they reached the surface—

"How do you like falling in?" said the prince.

After some effort the princess panted out,—

"Is that what you call *falling in*?"

"Yes," answered the prince, "I should think it a very tolerable specimen."

"It seemed to me like going up," rejoined she.

"My feeling was certainly one of elevation too," the prince conceded.

The princess did not appear to understand him, for she retorted his question:—

"How do *you* like falling in?" said the princess.

"Beyond everything," answered he; "for I have fallen in with the only perfect creature I ever saw."

"No more of that: I am tired of it," said the princess.

Perhaps she shared her father's aversion to punning.

"Don't you like falling in then?" said the prince.

"It is the most delightful fun I ever had in my life," answered she. "I never fell before. I wish I could learn. To think I am the only person in my father's kingdom that can't fall!"

Here the poor princess looked almost sad.

"I shall be most happy to fall in with you any time you like," said the prince, devotedly.

"Thank you. I don't know. Perhaps it would not be proper. But I don't care. At all events, as we have fallen in, let us have a swim together."

"With all my heart," responded the prince.

And away they went, swimming, and diving, and floating, until at last they heard cries along the shore, and saw lights glancing in all directions. It was now quite late, and there was no moon.

"I must go home," said the princess. "I am very sorry, for this is delightful."

"So am I," returned the prince. "But I am glad I haven't a home to go to—at least, I don't exactly know where it is."

"I wish I hadn't one either," rejoined the princess; "it is so stupid! I have a great mind," she continued, "to play them all a trick. Why couldn't they leave me alone? They won't trust me in the lake for a single night!—You see where that green light is burning? That is the window of my room. Now if you would just swim there with me very quietly, and when we are all but under the balcony, give me such a push—up you call it—as you did a little while ago, I should be able to catch hold of the balcony, and get in at the window; and then they may look for me till to-morrow morning!"

"With more obedience than pleasure," said the prince, gallantly; and away they swam, very gently.

"Will you be in the lake to-morrow night?" the prince ventured to ask.

"To be sure I will. I don't think so. Perhaps," was the princess's somewhat strange answer.

But the prince was intelligent enough not to press her further; and merely whispered, as he gave her the parting lift, "Don't tell."

The only answer the princess returned was a roguish look. She was already a yard above his head. The look seemed to say, "Never fear. It is too good fun to spoil that way."

So perfectly like other people had she been in the water, that even yet the prince could scarcely believe his eyes when he saw her ascend slowly, grasp the balcony, and disappear through the window. He turned, almost expecting to see her still by his side. But he was alone in the water. So he swam away quietly, and watched the lights roving about the shore for hours after the princess was safe in her chamber. As soon as they disappeared, he landed in search of his tunic and sword, and, after some trouble, found them again. Then he made the best of his way round the lake to the other side. There the wood was wilder, and the shore steeper-rising more immediately towards the mountains which surrounded the lake on all sides, and kept sending it messages of silvery streams from morning to night, and all night long. He soon found a spot whence he could see the green light in the princess's room, and where, even in the broad daylight, he would be in no danger of being discovered from the opposite shore. It was a sort of cave in the rock, where he provided himself a bed of withered leaves, and lay down too tired for hunger to keep him awake. All night long he dreamed that he was swimming with the princess.

10.

Look at the Moon.

Early the next morning the prince set out to look for something to eat, which he soon found at a forester's hut, where for many following days he was supplied with all that a brave prince could consider necessary. And having plenty to keep him alive for the present, he would not think of wants not yet in existence. Whenever Care intruded, this prince always bowed him out in the most princely manner. When he returned from his breakfast to his watch-cave, he saw the princess already floating about in the lake, attended by the king and queen whom he knew by their crowns—and a great company in lovely little boats, with canopies of all the colours of the rainbow, and flags and streamers of a great many more. It was a very bright day, and soon the prince, burned up with the heat, began to long for the cold water and the cool princess. But he had to endure till twilight; for the boats had provisions on board, and it was not till the sun went down that the gay party began to vanish. Boat after boat drew away to the shore, following that of the king and queen, till only one, apparently the princess's own boat, remained. But she did not want to go home even yet, and the prince thought he saw her order the boat to the shore without her. At all events, it rowed away; and now, of all the radiant company, only one white speck remained. Then the prince began to sing. And this is what he sung:—

> *"Lady fair,*
> *Swan-white,*
> *Lift thine eyes,*
> *Banish night*
> *By the might*
> *Of thine eyes.*
>
> *Snowy arms,*
> *Oars of snow,*
> *Oar her hither,*
> *Plashing low.*
> *Soft and slow,*
> *Oar her hither.*
>
> *Stream behind her*
> *O'er the lake,*
> *Radiant whiteness!*
> *In her wake*
> *Following, following for her sake.*
> *Radiant whiteness!*
>
> *Cling about her,*
> *Waters blue;*
> *Part not from her,*
> *But renew*
> *Cold and true*

Kisses round her.

Lap me round,
Waters sad,
That have left her.
Make me glad,
For ye had
Kissed her ere ye left her."

Before he had finished his song, the princess was just under the place where he sat, and looking up to find him. Her ears had led her truly.

"Would you like a fall, princess?" said the prince, looking down.

"Ah! there you are! Yes, if you please, prince," said the princess, looking up.

"How do you know I am a prince, princess?" said the prince.

"Because you are a very nice young man, prince," said the princess.

"Come up then, princess."

"Fetch me, prince."

The prince took off his scarf, then his sword-belt, then his tunic, and tied them all together, and let them down. But the line was far too short. He unwound his turban, and added it to the rest, when it was all but long enough; and his purse completed it. The princess just managed to lay hold of the knot of money, and was beside him in a moment. This rock was much higher than the other, and the splash and the dive were tremendous. The princess was in ecstasies of delight, and their swim was delicious.

Night after night they met, and swam about in the dark clear lake; where such was the prince's gladness, that (whether the princess's way of looking at things infected him, or he was actually getting light-headed) he often fancied that he was swimming in the sky instead of the lake. But when he talked about being in heaven, the princess laughed at him dreadfully.

When the moon came, she brought them fresh pleasure. Everything looked strange and new in her light, with an old, withered, yet unfading newness. When the moon was nearly full, one of their great delights was, to dive deep in the water, and then, turning round, look up through it at the great blot of light close above them, shimmering and trembling and wavering, spreading and contracting, seeming to melt away, and again grow solid. Then they would shoot up through the blot; and lo! there was the moon, far off, clear and steady and cold, and very lovely, at the bottom of a deeper and bluer lake than theirs, as the princess said.

The prince soon found out that while in the water the princess was very like other people. And besides this, she was not so forward in her questions or pert in her replies at sea as on shore. Neither did she laugh so much; and when she did laugh, it was more gently. She seemed altogether more modest and maidenly in the water than out of it.

But when the prince, who had really fallen in love when he fell in the lake, began to talk to her about love, she always turned her head towards him and laughed. After a while she began to look puzzled, as if she were trying to understand what he meant, but could not—revealing a notion that he meant something. But as soon as ever she left the lake, she was so altered, that the prince said to himself, "If I marry her, I see no help for it: we must turn merman and mermaid, and go out to sea at once."

11.

Hiss!

The princess's pleasure in the lake had grown to a passion, and she could scarcely bear to be out of it for an hour. Imagine then her consternation, when, diving with the prince one night, a sudden suspicion seized her that the lake was not so deep as it used to be. The prince could not imagine what had happened. She shot to the surface, and, without a word, swam at full speed towards the higher side of the lake. He followed, begging to know if she was ill, or what was the matter. She never turned her head, or took the smallest notice of his question. Arrived at the shore, she coasted the rocks with minute inspection. But she was not able to come to a conclusion, for the moon was very small, and so she could not see well. She turned therefore and swam home, without saying a word to explain her conduct to the prince, of whose presence she seemed no longer conscious. He withdrew to his cave, in great perplexity and distress.

Next day she made many observations, which, alas! strengthened her fears. She saw that the banks were too dry; and that the grass on the shore, and the trailing plants on the rocks, were withering away. She caused marks to be made along the borders, and examined them, day after day, in all directions of the wind; till at last the horrible idea became a certain fact—that the surface of the lake was slowly sinking.

The poor princess nearly went out of the little mind she had. It was awful to her to see the lake, which she loved more than any living thing, lie dying before her eyes. It sank away, slowly vanishing. The tops of rocks that had never been seen till now, began to appear far down in the clear water. Before long they were dry in the sun. It was fearful to think of the mud that would soon lie there baking and festering, full of lovely creatures dying, and ugly creatures coming to life, like the unmaking of a world. And how hot the sun would be without any lake! She could not bear to swim in it any more, and began to pine away. Her life seemed bound up with it; and ever as the lake sank, she pined. People said she would not live an hour after the lake was gone.

But she never cried.

A Proclamation was made to all the kingdom, that whosoever should discover the cause of the lake's decrease, would be rewarded after a princely fashion. Hum-Drum and Kopy-Keck applied themselves to their physics and metaphysics; but in vain. Not even they could suggest a cause.

Now the fact was that the old princess was at the root of the mischief. When she heard that her niece found more pleasure in the water than any one else out of it, she went into a rage, and cursed herself for her want of foresight.

"But," said she, "I will soon set all right. The king and the people shall die of thirst; their brains shall boil and frizzle in their skulls before I will lose my revenge."

And she laughed a ferocious laugh, that made the hairs on the back of her black cat stand erect with terror.

Then she went to an old chest in the room, and opening it, took out what looked like a piece of dried seaweed. This she threw into a tub of water. Then she threw some powder into the water, and stirred it with her bare arm, muttering over it words of hideous sound, and yet more hideous import. Then she set the tub aside, and took from the chest a huge bunch of a hundred rusty keys, that clattered in her shaking hands. Then she sat down and proceeded to oil them all. Before she had finished, out from the tub, the water of which had kept on a slow motion ever since she had ceased stirring it, came the head and half the body of a huge gray snake. But the witch did not look round. It grew out of the tub, waving itself backwards and forwards with a slow horizontal motion, till it reached the princess, when it laid its head upon her shoulder, and gave a low hiss in her ear. She started—but with joy; and seeing the head resting on her shoulder, drew it towards her and kissed it. Then she drew it all out of the tub, and wound it round her body. It was one of those dreadful creatures which few have ever beheld—the White Snakes of Darkness.

Then she took the keys and went down to her cellar; and as she unlocked the door she said to herself,—

"This *is* worth living for!"

Locking the door behind her, she descended a few steps into the cellar, and crossing it, unlocked another door into a dark, narrow passage. She locked this also behind her, and descended a few more steps. If any one had followed the witch-princess, he would have heard her unlock exactly one hundred doors, and descend a few steps after unlocking each. When she had unlocked the last, she entered a vast cave, the roof of which was supported by huge natural pillars of rock. Now this roof was the under side of the bottom of the lake.

She then untwined the snake from her body, and held it by the tail high above her. The hideous creature stretched up its head towards the roof of the cavern, which it was just able to reach. It then began to move its head backwards and forwards, with a slow oscillating motion, as if looking for something. At the same moment the witch began to walk round and round the cavern, coming nearer to the centre every circuit; while the head of the snake described the same path over the roof that she did over the floor, for she kept holding it up. And still it kept slowly oscillating. Round and round the cavern they went, ever lessening the circuit, till at last the snake made a sudden dart, and clung to the roof with its mouth.

"That's right, my beauty!" cried the princess; "drain it dry."

She let it go, left it hanging, and sat down on a great stone, with her black cat, which had followed her all round the cave, by her side. Then she began to knit and mutter awful words. The snake hung like a huge leech, sucking at the stone; the cat stood with his back arched, and his tail like a piece of cable, looking up at the snake; and the old woman sat and knitted and muttered. Seven days and seven nights they remained thus; when suddenly the serpent dropped from the roof as if exhausted, and shrivelled up till it was again like a piece of dried seaweed. The witch started to her feet, picked it up, put it in her pocket, and looked up at the roof. One drop of water was trembling on the spot where the snake had been sucking. As soon as she saw that, she turned and fled, followed by her cat. Shutting the door in a terrible hurry, she locked it, and having muttered some frightful words, sped to the next, which also she locked and muttered over; and so with all the hundred doors, till she arrived in her own cellar. Then she sat down on the floor ready to faint, but listening with malicious delight to the rushing of the water, which she could hear distinctly through all the hundred doors.

But this was not enough. Now that she had tasted revenge, she lost her patience. Without further measures, the lake would be too long in disappearing. So the next night, with the last shred of the dying old moon rising, she took some of the water in which she had revived the snake, put it in a bottle, and set out, accompanied by her cat. Before morning she had made the entire circuit of the lake, muttering fearful words as she crossed every stream, and casting into it some of the water out of her bottle. When she had finished the circuit she muttered yet again, and flung a handful of water towards the moon. Thereupon every spring in the country ceased to throb and bubble, dying away like the pulse of a dying man. The next day there was no sound of falling water to be heard along the borders of the lake. The very courses were dry; and the mountains showed no silvery streaks down their dark sides.

And not alone had the fountains of mother Earth ceased to flow; for all the babies throughout the country were crying dreadfully—only without tears.

12.

Where Is the Prince?

Never since the night when the princess left him so abruptly had the prince had a single interview with her. He had seen her once or twice in the lake; but as far as he could discover, she had not been in it any more at night. He had sat and sung, and looked in vain for his Nereid; while she, like a true Nereid, was wasting away with her lake, sinking as it sank, withering as it dried. When at length he discovered the change that was taking place in the level of the water, he was in great alarm and perplexity. He could not tell whether the lake was dying because the lady had forsaken it; or whether the lady would not come because the lake had begun to sink. But he resolved to know so much at least.

He disguised himself, and, going to the palace, requested to see the lord chamberlain. His appearance at once gained his request; and the lord chamberlain, being a man of some insight, perceived that there was more in the prince's solicitation than met the ear. He felt likewise that no one could tell whence a solution of the present difficulties might arise. So he granted the prince's prayer to be made shoeblack to the princess. It was rather cunning in the prince to request such an easy post, for the princess could not possibly soil as many shoes as other princesses.

He soon learned all that could be told about the princess. He went nearly distracted; but after roaming about the lake for days, and diving in every depth that remained, all that he could do was to put an extra polish on the dainty pair of boots that was never called for.

For the princess kept her room, with the curtains drawn to shut out the dying lake, But she could not shut it out of her mind for a moment. It haunted her imagination so that she felt as if the lake were her soul, drying up within her, first to mud, then to madness and death. She thus brooded over the change, with all its dreadful accompaniments, till she was nearly distracted. As for the prince, she had forgotten him. However much she had enjoyed his company in the water, she did not care for him without it. But she seemed to have forgotten her father and mother too. The lake went on sinking. Small slimy spots began to appear, which glittered steadily amidst the changeful shine of the water. These grew to broad patches of mud, which widened and spread, with rocks here and there, and floundering fishes and crawling eels swarming. The people went everywhere catching these, and looking for anything that might have dropped from the royal boats.

At length the lake was all but gone, only a few of the deepest pools remaining unexhausted.

It happened one day that a party of youngsters found themselves on the brink of one of these pools in the very centre of the lake. it was a rocky basin of considerable depth. Looking in, they saw at the bottom something that shone yellow in the sun. A little boy jumped in and dived for it. It was a plate of gold covered with writing. They carried it to the king. On one side of it stood these words:—

> *"Death alone from death can save.*
> *Love is death, and so is brave—*
> *Love can fill the deepest grave.*
> *Love loves on beneath the wave."*

Now this was enigmatical enough to the king and courtiers. But the reverse of the plate explained it a little. Its writing amounted to this:—

"If the lake should disappear, they must find the hole through which the water ran. But it would be useless to try to stop it by any ordinary means. There was but one effectual mode.—The body of a living man could alone stanch the flow. The man must give himself of his own will; and the lake must take his life as it filled. Otherwise the offering would be of no avail. If the nation could not provide one hero, it was time it should perish."

13.

Here I Am.

This was a very disheartening revelation to the king—not that he was unwilling to sacrifice a subject, but that he was hopeless of finding a man willing to sacrifice himself. No time was to be lost, however, for the princess was lying motionless on her bed, and taking no nourishment but lake-water, which was now none of the best. Therefore the king caused the contents of the wonderful plate of gold to be published throughout the country.

No one, however, came forward.

The prince, having gone several days' journey into the forest, to consult a hermit whom he had met there on his way to Lagobel, knew nothing of the oracle till his return.

When he had acquainted himself with all the particulars, he sat down and thought,—

"She will die if I don't do it, and life would be nothing to me without her; so I shall lose nothing by doing it. And life will be as pleasant to her as ever, for she will soon forget me. And there will be so much more beauty and happiness in the world!—To be sure, I shall not see it." (Here the poor prince gave a sigh.) "How lovely the lake will be in the moonlight, with that glorious creature sporting in it like a wild goddess!— It is rather hard to be drowned by inches, though. Let me see—that will be seventy inches of me to drown." (Here he tried to laugh, but could not.) "The longer the better, however," he resumed: "for can I not bargain that the princess shall be beside me all the time? So I shall see her once more, kiss her perhaps,—who knows?—and die looking in her eyes. It will be no death. At least, I shall not feel it. And to see the lake filling for the beauty again!—All right! I am ready."

He kissed the princess's boot, laid it down, and hurried to the king's apartment. But feeling, as he went, that anything sentimental would be disagreeable, he resolved to carry off the whole affair with nonchalance. So he knocked at the door of the king's counting-house, where it was all but a capital crime to disturb him.

When the king heard the knock he started up, and opened the door in a rage. Seeing only the shoeblack, he drew his sword. This, I am sorry to say, was his usual mode of asserting his regality when he thought his dignity was in danger. But the prince was not in the least alarmed.

"Please your Majesty, I'm your butler," said he.

"My butler! you lying rascal! What do you mean?"

"I mean, I will cork your big bottle."

"Is the fellow mad?" bawled the king, raising the point of his sword.

"I will put a stopper—plug—what you call it, in your leaky lake, grand monarch," said the prince.

The king was in such a rage that before he could speak he had time to cool, and to reflect that it would be great waste to kill the only man who was willing to be useful in the present emergency, seeing that in the end the insolent fellow would be as dead as if he had died by his Majesty's own hand. "Oh!" said he at last, putting up his sword with difficulty, it was so long; "I am obliged to you, you young fool! Take a glass of wine?"

'No, thank you," replied the prince.

"Very well," said the king. "Would you like to run and see your parents before you make your experiment?"

"No, thank you," said the prince.

"Then we will go and look for the hole at once," said his Majesty, and proceeded to call some attendants.

"Stop, please your Majesty; I have a condition to make," interposed the prince.

"What!" exclaimed the king, "a condition! and with me! How dare you?"

"As you please," returned the prince, coolly. "I wish your Majesty a good morning."

"You wretch! I will have you put in a sack, and stuck in the hole."

"Very well, your Majesty," replied the prince, becoming a little more respectful, lest the wrath of the king should deprive him of the pleasure of dying for the princess. "But what good will that do your Majesty? Please to remember that the oracle says the victim must offer himself."

"Well, you *have* offered yourself," retorted the king.

"Yes, upon one condition."

"Condition again!" roared the king, once more drawing his sword. "Begone! Somebody else will be glad enough to take the honour off your shoulders."

"Your Majesty knows it will not be easy to get another to take my place."

"Well, what is your condition?" growled the king, feeling that the prince was right.

"Only this," replied the prince: "that, as I must on no account die before I am fairly drowned, and the waiting will be rather wearisome, the princess, your daughter, shall go with me, feed me with her own hands, and look at me now and then to comfort me; for you must confess it IS rather hard. As soon as the water is up to my eyes, she may go and be happy, and forget her poor shoeblack."

Here the prince's voice faltered, and he very nearly grew sentimental, in spite of his resolution.

"Why didn't you tell me before what your condition was? Such a fuss about nothing!" exclaimed the king.

"Do you grant it?" persisted the prince. "Of course I do," replied the king.

"Very well. I am ready."

"Go and have some dinner, then, while I set my people to find the place."

The king ordered out his guards, and gave directions to the officers to find the hole in the lake at once. So the bed of the lake was marked out in divisions and thoroughly examined, and in an hour or so the hole was discovered. It was in the middle of a stone, near the centre of the lake, in the very pool where the golden plate had been found. It was a three-cornered hole of no great size. There was water all round the stone, but very little was flowing through the hole.

14.

This Is Very Kind of You.

The prince went to dress for the occasion, for he was resolved to die like a prince.

When the princess heard that a man had offered to die for her, she was so transported that she jumped off the bed, feeble as she was, and danced about the room for joy. She did not care who the man was; that was nothing to her. The hole wanted stopping; and if only a man would do, why, take one. In an hour or two more everything was ready. Her maid dressed her in haste, and they carried her to the side of the lake. When she saw it she shrieked, and covered her face with her hands. They bore her across to the stone where they had already placed a little boat for her.

The water was not deep enough to float it, but they hoped it would be, before long. They laid her on cushions, placed in the boat wines and fruits and other nice things, and stretched a canopy over all.

In a few minutes the prince appeared. The princess recognized him at once, but did not think it worth while to acknowledge him.

"Here I am," said the prince. "Put me in."

"They told me it was a shoeblack," said the princess.

"So I am," said the prince. "I blacked your little boots three times a day, because they were all I could get of you. Put me in."

The courtiers did not resent his bluntness, except by saying to each other that he was taking it out in impudence.

But how was he to be put in? The golden plate contained no instructions on this point. The prince looked at the hole, and saw but one way. He put both his legs into it, sitting on the stone, and, stooping forward, covered the corner that remained open with his two hands. In this uncomfortable position he resolved to abide his fate, and turning to the people, said,—

"Now you can go."

The king had already gone home to dinner.

"Now you can go," repeated the princess after him, like a parrot.

The people obeyed her and went.

Presently a little wave flowed over the stone, and wetted one of the prince's knees. But he did not mind it much. He began to sing, and the song he sang was this:—

"As a world that has no well,
Darting bright in forest dell;
As a world without the gleam
Of the downward-going stream;
As a world without the glance
Of the ocean's fair expanse;
As a world where never rain
Glittered on the sunny plain;—
Such, my heart, thy world would be,
If no love did flow in thee.

As a world without the sound
Of the rivulets underground;
Or the bubbling of the spring
Out of darkness wandering;
Or the mighty rush and flowing
Of the river's downward going;
Or the music-showers that drop
On the outspread beech's top;
Or the ocean's mighty voice,
When his lifted waves rejoice;—
Such, my soul, thy world would be,
If no love did sing in thee.

> *Lady, keep thy world's delight;*
> *Keep the waters in thy sight.*
> *Love hath made me strong to go,*
> *For thy sake, to realms below,*
> *Where the water's shine and hum*
> *Through the darkness never come;*
> *Let, I pray, one thought of me*
> *Spring, a little well, in thee;*
> *Lest thy loveless soul be found*
> *Like a dry and thirsty ground."*

"Sing again, prince. It makes it less tedious," said the princess.

But the prince was too much overcome to sing any more, and a long pause followed.

"This is very kind of you, prince," said the princess at last, quite coolly, as she lay in the boat with her eyes shut.

"I am sorry I can't return the compliment," thought the prince; "but you are worth dying for, after all."

Again a wavelet, and another, and another flowed over the stone, and wetted both the prince's knees; but he did not speak or move. Two—three—four hours passed in this way, the princess apparently asleep, and the prince very patient. But he was much disappointed in his position, for he had none of the consolation he had hoped for.

At last he could bear it no longer.

"Princess!" said he.

But at the moment up started the princess, crying,—

"I'm afloat! I'm afloat!"

And the little boat bumped against the stone.

"Princess!" repeated the prince, encouraged by seeing her wide awake and looking eagerly at the water.

"Well?" said she, without looking round.

"Your papa promised that you should look at me, and you haven't looked at me once."

"Did he? Then I suppose I must. But I am so sleepy!"

"Sleep then, darling, and don't mind me," said the poor prince.

"Really, you are very good," replied the princess. "I think I will go to sleep again."

"Just give me a glass of wine and a biscuit first," said the prince, very humbly.

"With all my heart," said the princess, and gaped as she said it.

She got the wine and the biscuit, however, and leaning over the side of the boat towards him, was compelled to look at him.

"Why, prince," she said, "you don't look well! Are you sure you don't mind it?" "Not a bit," answered he, feeling very faint in deed. "Only I shall die before it is of any use to you, unless I have something to eat."

"There, then," said she, holding out the wine to him.

"Ah! you must feed me. I dare not move my hands. The water would run away directly."

"Good gracious!" said the princess; and she began at once to feed him with bits of biscuit and sips of wine.

As she fed him, he contrived to kiss the tips of her fingers now and then. She did not seem to mind it, one way or the other. But the prince felt better.

"Now for your own sake, princess," said he, "I cannot let you go to sleep. You must sit and look at me, else I shall not be able to keep up."

"Well, I will do anything I can to oblige you," answered she, with condescension; and, sitting down, she did look at him, and kept looking at him with wonderful steadiness, considering all things.

The sun went down, and the moon rose, and, gush after gush, the waters were rising up the prince's body. They were up to his waist now.

"Why can't we go and have a swim?" said the princess. "There seems to be water enough Just about here."

"I shall never swim more," said the prince.

"Oh, I forgot," said the princess, and was silent.

So the water grew and grew, and rose up and up on the prince. And the princess sat and looked at him. She fed him now and then. The night wore on. The waters rose and rose. The moon rose likewise higher and higher, and shone full on the face of the dying prince. The water was up to his neck.

"Will you kiss me, princess?" said he, feebly.

The nonchalance was all gone now.

"Yes, I will," answered the princess, and kissed him with a long, sweet, cold kiss.

"Now," said he, with a sigh of content, "I die happy."

He did not speak again. The princess gave him some wine for the last time: he was past eating. Then she sat down again, and looked at him. The water rose and rose. It touched his chin. It touched his lower lip. It touched between his lips. He shut them hard to keep it out. The princess began to feel strange. It touched his upper lip. He breathed through his nostrils. The princess looked wild. It covered his nostrils. Her eyes looked scared, and shone strange in the moonlight. His head fell back; the water closed over it, and the bubbles of his last breath bubbled up through the water. The princess gave a shriek, and sprang into the lake.

She laid hold first of one leg, and then of the other, and pulled and tugged, but she could not move either. She stopped to take breath, and that made her think that *he* could not get any breath. She was frantic. She got hold of him, and held his head above the water, which was possible now his hands were no longer on the hole. But it was of no use, for he was past breathing.

Love and water brought back all her strength. She got under the water, and pulled and pulled with her whole might, till at last she got one leg out. The other easily followed. How she got him into the boat she never could tell; but when she did, she fainted away. Coming to herself, she seized the oars, kept herself steady as best she could, and rowed and rowed, though she had never rowed before. Round rocks, and over shallows, and through mud she rowed, till she got to the landing- stairs of the palace. By this time her people were on the shore, for they had heard her shriek. She made them carry the prince to her own room, and lay him in her bed, and light a fire, and send for the doctors.

"But the lake, your Highness!" said the chamberlain, who, roused by the noise, came in, in his nightcap.

"Go and drown yourself in it!" she said.

This was the last rudeness of which the princess was ever guilty; and one must allow that she had good cause to feel provoked with the lord chamberlain.

Had it been the king himself, he would have fared no better. But both he and the queen were fast asleep. And the chamberlain went back to his bed. Somehow, the doctors never came. So the princess and her old nurse were left with the prince. But the old nurse was a wise woman, and knew what to do.

They tried everything for a long time without success. The princess was nearly distracted between hope and fear, but she tried on and on, one thing after another, and everything over and over again.

At last, when they had all but given it up, just as the sun rose, the prince opened his eyes.

15.

Look at the Rain!

The princess burst into a passion of tears, and *fell* on the floor. There she lay for an hour, and her tears never ceased. All the pent-up crying of her life was spent now. And a rain came on, such as had never been seen in that country. The sun shone all the time, and the great drops, which fell straight to the earth, shone likewise. The palace was in the heart of a rainbow. It was a rain of rubies, and sapphires, and emeralds, and topazes. The torrents poured from the mountains like molten gold; and if it had not been for its subterraneous outlet, the lake would have overflowed and inundated the country. It was full from shore to shore.

But the princess did not heed the lake. She lay on the floor and wept, and this rain within doors was far more wonderful than the rain out of doors.

For when it abated a little, and she proceeded to rise, she found, to her astonishment, that she could not. At length, after many efforts, she succeeded in getting upon her feet. But she tumbled down again directly. Hearing her fall, her old nurse uttered a yell of delight, and ran to her, screaming,—

"My darling child! she's found her gravity!"

"Oh, that's it! is it?" said the princess, rubbing her shoulder and her knee alternately. "I consider it very unpleasant. I feel as if I should be crushed to pieces."

"Hurrah!" cried the prince from the bed. "If you've come round, princess, so have I. How's the lake?"

"Brimful," answered the nurse.

"Then we're all happy."

"That we are indeed!" answered the princess, sobbing.

And there was rejoicing all over the country that rainy day. Even the babies forgot their past troubles, and danced and crowed amazingly. And the king told stories, and the queen listened to them. And he divided the money in his box, and she the honey in her pot, among all the children. And there was such jubilation as was never heard of before.

Of course the prince and princess were betrothed at once. But the princess had to learn to walk, before they could be married with any propriety. And this was not so easy at her time of life, for she could walk no more than a baby. She was always falling down and hurting herself.

"Is this the gravity you used to make so much of?" said she one day to the prince, as he raised her from the floor. "For my part, I was a great deal more comfortable without it."

"No, no, that's not it. This is it," replied the prince, as he took her up, and carried her about like a baby, kissing her all the time. "This is gravity."

"That's better," said she. "I don't mind that so much."

And she smiled the sweetest, loveliest smile in the prince's face. And she gave him one little kiss in return for all his; and he thought them overpaid, for he was beside himself with delight. I fear she complained of her gravity more than once after this, notwithstanding.

It was a long time before she got reconciled to walking. But the pain of learning it was quite counterbalanced by two things, either of which would have been sufficient consolation. The first was, that the prince himself was her teacher; and the second, that she could tumble into the lake as often as she pleased. Still, she preferred to have the prince jump in with her; and the splash they made before was nothing to the splash they made now.

The lake never sank again. In process of time, it wore the roof of the cavern quite through, and was twice as deep as before.

The only revenge the princess took upon her aunt was to tread pretty hard on her gouty toe the next time she saw her. But she was sorry for it the very next day, when she heard that the water had undermined her house, and that it had fallen in the night, burying her in its ruins; whence no one ever ventured to dig up her body. There she lies to this day.

So the prince and princess lived and were happy; and had crowns of gold, and clothes of cloth, and shoes of leather, and children of boys and girls, not one of whom was ever known, on the most critical occasion, to lose the smallest atom of his or her due proportion of gravity.

THE END

CPSIA information can be obtained at www.ICGtesting.com
Printed in the USA
BVOW04s1559220114

342669BV00001B/71/P